Living things

One day, Jenny saw Timmy jumping on some ants. 'Stop! Don't hurt the ants! They are living things!' said Jenny.

'What are living things?' asked Timmy.

'All things that are alive are called living things. Living things can breathe and eat and move about,' said Jenny.

'Do you know why an ant is a living thing?
Because it eats sugar and can move about!'

'Wow!' said Timmy. Jenny and Timmy watched the ants crawl on the ground.

'Is my dog Lolo a living thing?' asked Timmy.

'Yes!' said Jenny, 'Lolo can run and jump and eat. And Lolo can bark!'

'Woof! Woof!' barked Lolo, happily.

Timmy saw a bird fly by. 'Is that bird a living thing?' he asked.

'Yes, a bird is a living thing too! Look how it flies in the sky.' said Jenny. They watched the beautiful bird fly over the trees.

Jenny pointed at a tree. She said, 'A tree is a living thing too! It breathes air and drinks water from the ground.'

'And trees are living things because they grow big too!' said Timmy. Jenny and Timmy clapped happily.

'All plants and animals are living things,' said Jenny.

'So that means all the squirrels and trees and people are living things!' said Timmy.

'And do you know what else is a living thing?' asked Jenny.

'Yes!' said Timmy, 'I am a living thing! And you are a living thing too, Jenny!' Timmy was so happy that he did a little dance.

'Woof! Woof!' barked Lolo. 'I love being a living thing!' said Timmy.

One day, Timmy said to Jenny, 'I know that all those things that are alive are living things. But what are non-living things?'

'Non-living things are all those things that are not alive. They do not eat or grow or move about on their own. And non-living things do not give birth to babies,' said Jenny.

Then Jenny and Timmy went out for a walk.

Timmy and Jenny saw a tree. 'Look at that tree. It has grown bigger than it was last year,' said Jenny.

Jenny picked up a stone and asked, 'But this stone stayed the same size. Why did the stone not grow?'

Timmy replied, 'Because a stone is a non-living thing. And non-living things do not grow!'

21

Then Jenny and Timmy went out to the park.
They watched their friends play football.

'When you kick the football, it does not get hurt,' said Jenny, 'That is because a football is a non-living thing. And non-living things do not get hurt.'

A little bird flew above their heads. 'A bird can move about on its own. But what about this bottle, can it move about on its own?' asked Jenny.

'No,' said Timmy, 'That is because bottles are non-living things. Non-living things cannot move about on their own.'

Next, the children soon saw a squirrel. Timmy threw a few nuts to the squirrel. The squirrel quickly ate up the nuts. 'A squirrel eats nuts. A mouse eats cheese. But does this bench eat anything?' asked Jenny.

'No,' replied Timmy, 'The bench does not eat anything. That is because it is a non-living thing. Non-living things do not eat anything!'

Soon Jenny and Timmy saw a herd of cows. 'Moo moo!' said the cows.

'A bird sings, a cow moos, and a lion roars. But a hat makes no sounds,' said Jenny. 'It is because a hat is a non-living thing. And non-living things cannot make sounds.'

Jenny and Timmy saw a cat with her kittens.

Jenny said, 'A cat gives birth to kittens. A duck gives birth to ducklings. But a gate does not give birth to baby gates.'

'Yes,' replied Timmy, 'That is because a gate is a non-living thing. And non-living things cannot give birth!'

At the end of the day,
Timmy said, 'Thanks
for teaching me about
non-living things, Jenny.
You're the best!' Both
Timmy and Jenny were
very happy.